OCTONAUTS ™

and the
WHITETIP SHARK

GROSSET & DUNLAP
Published by the Penguin Group
Penguin Group (USA) LLC, 375 Hudson Street, New York, New York 10014, USA

USA | Canada | UK | Ireland | Australia | New Zealand | India | South Africa | China

penguin.com
A Penguin Random House Company

ISBN 978-0-448-48439-6   10 9 8 7 6 5 4 3 2 1

MEET THE CREW!

The daring crew of the Octopod are ready
to embark on an exciting new mission!

INKLING
(Professor)

KWAZII
(Lieutenant)

PESO
(Medic)

BARNACLES
(Captain)

TWEAK
(Engineer)

SHELLINGTON
(Field Researcher)

DASHI
(Photographer)

TUNIP
(Ship's Cook)

EXPLORE . RESCUE . PROTECT

OCTONAUTS

AND THE
WHITETIP SHARK

Grosset & Dunlap
An Imprint of Penguin Group (USA) LLC

Captain Barnacles had an exciting new mission for the Octonauts.
"We need to find out what kind of sharks visit this reef," he announced.
Shellington grinned. He couldn't wait to study a shark up close!
"Not too close." Peso gulped.
"Sharks can be dangerous."

Kwazii grinned. "And that's why I can't wait to get going and . . ."

"Clean the GUPs?" Captain Barnacles asked. "Our GUPs are covered in gunk, and they don't work well when they're dirty."

"Aye, aye," groaned Kwazii. "But I'd rather be swimming with the sharks!"

Barnacles, Peso, and Shellington climbed aboard the GUP-A.

The GUP-A chugged through the ocean.
A stripy fish peeped out of the shadows.
"Look! There's a pilot fish," said
Shellington. "No sharks though."
"Let's move farther down the reef,"
said Captain Barnacles.
No one noticed the
pilot fish dart up
and nibble at the
bottom of
the GUP-A.

Peso and Shellington watched and waited. There didn't seem to be any sharks around.

"Try the front window," suggested Captain Barnacles.

"Jumping jellyfish!" cried Shellington.

A great big whitetip shark was swimming straight toward the GUP-A!

≡ FACT: WHITETIP SHARK

This type of shark has white tips on its fins.

The whitetip shark opened its massive mouth.
"Look at those teeth," remarked Shellington.
"It could use a toothbrush!"

Suddenly, the shark grabbed the GUP-A's light and thrashed its tail.
"What's he trying to do?" gasped Peso.
Shellington frowned. "He's trying to take a bite out of the GUP!"

"The shark could hurt himself and us," cried Captain
Barnacles. "Hold on!" Barnacles tried to get the GUP-A free
of the shark.

The whitetip shark chased the Octonauts. The little pilot
fish followed, too.

Put-put-put!

The GUP-A spluttered to a stop.

"Some gunk must have gotten into the propeller,"
said the captain.

Finally he got the GUP-A started again
and they pulled away just in time!

Back on the Octopod, Professor Inkling and Kwazii were playing table tennis.

"This is easier for you!" cried Kwazii, hitting the ball.

The professor laughed. Even with eight tentacles and four bats, Kwazii was impossible to beat.

Time was ticking away, and Kwazii was supposed to be cleaning the GUPs, but he was having too much fun.
"Just one more game," he said, "against all of you!"
Professor Inkling, Tweak, and Tunip grabbed their paddles.
"You're on!"

The table tennis match was getting exciting.
"The next point wins." Kwazii grinned.
He glanced out the window. Was that the GUP-A having a grand adventure chasing after a whitetip shark?

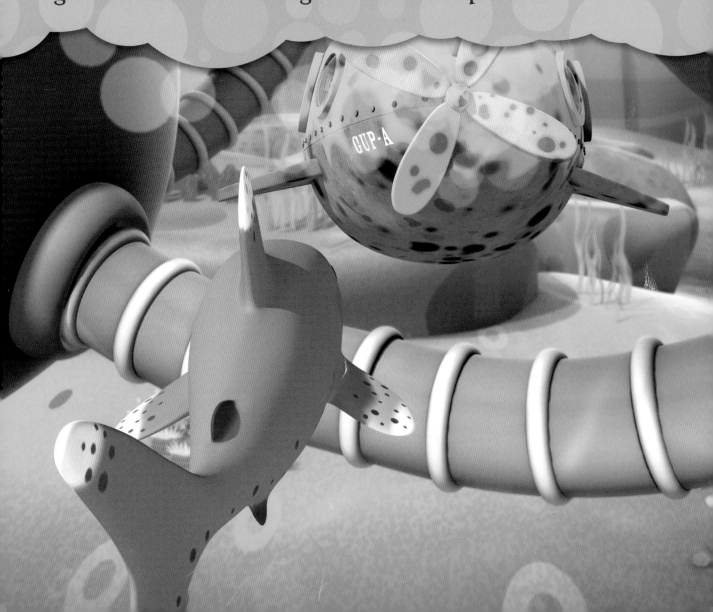

The Octonauts
peered through the glass.
"They're not chasing that shark,"
shouted Dashi. "That shark is chasing them!"
Not only was the shark chasing the GUP-A, it was starting
to catch up!
"We can't shake him," said the captain. "Peso, sound
the Octoalert!"

"Octonauts, to

Tweak opened the Octohatch. As soon as the GUP-A was in, she closed the door again, shutting the shark outside! The crew were relieved to be back in the launch bay.

"That will teach me to take out a gunky GUP," said the captain with a sigh. "How's the cleaning coming along, Kwazii?"
"I haven't started . . . I mean finished yet, Captain," admitted Kwazii.
Kwazii hurried back to work.

Kwazii jumped in the launch-bay pool.
One GUP already looked shiny and new.
"Who cleaned the GUP-E?" he
wondered aloud.

The pilot fish swam up. "I did!"
Kwazii blinked. "You like cleaning?"
"I live for it." The fish beamed.
"Eat and clean, clean and eat,
you know how it is!"
"Ha-ha!" laughed Kwazii.
"Dinner is served!"

⬱ FACT: PILOT FISH

Pilot fish get
their food by
eating gunk off
things.

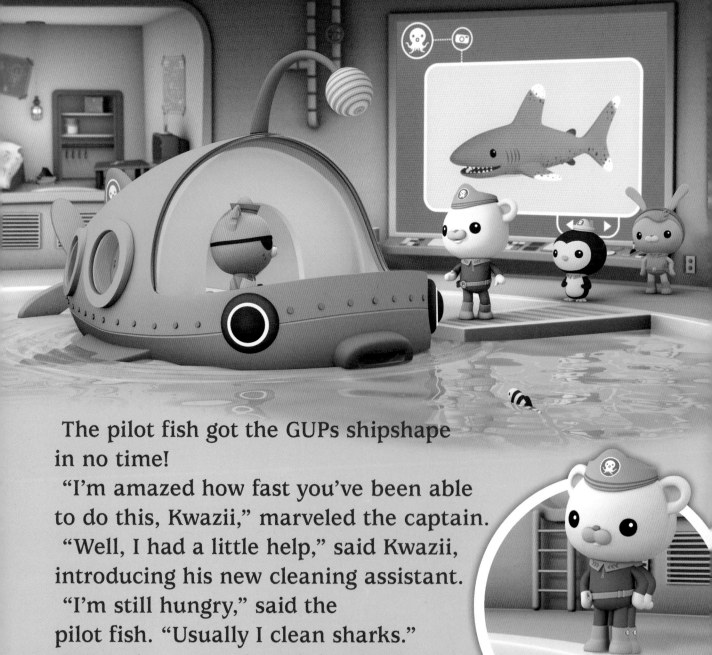

The pilot fish got the GUPs shipshape
in no time!
"I'm amazed how fast you've been able
to do this, Kwazii," marveled the captain.
"Well, I had a little help," said Kwazii,
introducing his new cleaning assistant.
"I'm still hungry," said the
pilot fish. "Usually I clean sharks."
Barnacles remembered the shark
on the reef. His teeth were very dirty.

The Octonauts decided to help the pilot fish find the whitetip shark.
 "Open the Octohatch!" cried Barnacles.
 Kwazii wasn't missing this mission. It definitely beat cleaning GUPs!

The pilot fish led the GUP-A back out to the reef.
"Oh!" Peso gasped. **"Sh-sh-shark!"**

The shark looked angry. It bit on the GUP-A's light, then snapped at the portholes. "Time to eat and clean," said the pilot fish. "Open wide, buddy!"

"Maybe this wasn't such a good idea," squeaked Peso. But instead of eating the pilot fish, the shark let him clean his teeth!

"That's better." The whitetip shark grinned.
"You're just the little fellow I need."
"Thanks, Octonauts!" shouted the pilot fish, swimming away with his new friend.

"I'm going to miss him." Kwazii sighed. "I'll have to clean the GUPs by myself next time."
The friends chuckled all the way back to the Octopod.

CAPTAIN'S LOG

Calling all Octonauts! Our mission to the reef was our most dangerous yet, but we learned something unusual. Who would have thought that a tiny pilot fish would make friends with a fierce whitetip shark?

CAPTAIN BARNACLES

FACT FILE: THE WHITETIP SHARK AND PILOT FISH

OCTOFACTS

Pilot fish and sharks help each other.

•

The pilot fish keeps the shark's teeth clean and the shark scares away other fish that might try to eat the pilot fish.

•

Sometimes a whole shoal of pilot fish will live and swim with one shark.

The pilot fish and whitetip shark have a special friendship called symbiosis. The pilot fish follows the shark wherever it goes, eating and cleaning the gunk from its teeth.

They live in the Sunlight Zone.

The shark eats fish and squid.

The pilot fish eats the shark's leftovers.

EXPLORE . RESCUE . PROTECT